SEVERN CULLIS-SUZUKI

TELL THE WORLD

A Young Environmentalist Speaks Out

DOUBLEDAY

Toronto   New York   London   Sydney   Auckland

CANADIAN CATALOGUING IN PUBLICATION DATA

Cullis-Suzuki, Severn
  Tell the world

ISBN 0-385-25422-9

1. Environmental protection.   2. Conservation of
natural resources.   3. Ecology.   I. Title.

TD170.C85 1993   363.7   C93-094203 5

Cover and text design by Tania Craan
Cover photograph by Barbara Woodley
Illustrations courtesy the students of
the Etobicoke School of the Arts and
Central Technical School, Ontario, Canada

Printed and bound in Mexico
Printed on recycled paper

Published in Canada by
Doubleday Canada Limited
105 Bond Street
Toronto, Ontario
M5B 1Y3

TELL THE WORLD

My name is Severn Cullis-Suzuki. I'm thirteen years old and I'm in Grade Eight at Kitsilano Secondary School in Vancouver, British Columbia, Canada. I'm involved in environmental issues because I love nature and consider it part of me and me part of it. I've gone camping ever since I was little, looking in creeks and exploring forests. Even in the city there are always squirrels, bugs or birds nearby. At home I live right on the ocean and the pools at low tide are full of sea creatures — blue herons, anemones, blennies, kelp, starfish and crabs.

I'm lucky to spend a lot of time with my grandparents. They've told me how different things were when they were my age, how much technology has changed the world, how our lifestyles have changed so much in comfort and progress. But many problems have come with these changes. Our resources are declining. Now the fish are fewer, the forests are decreasing and the air is becoming harder to breathe.

I have also learned a lot about environmental problems by travelling. I've gone to Brazil, Costa Rica and Ecuador and now I realize how lucky I am to live in Canada. We take so much for granted, the dinners on our tables, our education, medical help, jobs and even our futures. In so many developing countries, poor peoples' main worry is trying simply to

CHRISTINA LEE, AGE 14

Our

message

is that children

are the future,

and the mess

adults leave will

be *our* home

one day.

survive and to find food. Few people in developed countries realize just how lucky we are.

My parents have been activists for the environment for a long time and a lot of their projects involve fighting alongside Native people. From our many Native friends we have learned an attitude of respect towards the Earth. When I began to learn about our environmental problems, I felt I had to do something. But what could I do? I was just little. I started by selling lemonade and old books on the sidewalk. All the money went to the fight to save the Stein Valley in British Columbia from logging.

My lucky dad gets to travel all over to do TV shows. In 1989, he went to Brazil for three months to film a program about the Amazon rain forest. He was so affected by the situation there that later, he took me, my mom and my sister Sarika to visit. We lived in a Kayapo village called Aucre with our Kayapo friends in the heart of the Amazon jungle for ten days. The people of Aucre don't have a lot of possessions, but they fit into their world better than many people outside the forest do. They don't own clothes — *paint* is their clothing. They don't have supermarkets — the *river* is their grocery store. They don't have pharmacies, but the forest offers more cures and remedies than we will ever know.

It is one of the most wonderful places on Earth. We slept in hammocks in a mud hut in the village. We swam, ate turtle legs, watched dancing and singing, went fishing and exploring with our Kayapo friends.

But as I flew out of the vast green forest, I saw many parasites nibbling at the edges. Goldmines chewing up the land and poisoning the rivers with mercury, fire slicing through the forest and its smoke choking the sky and blacking out the sun. The Kayapo and their neighbours are caught in the centre of it all. The threat to my friends and to the animals and plants made me feel angry — and helpless. When I got back to Canada, I decided I had to help them. I was nine years old. At school, I told my friends about the Kayapo children and the danger they were in. Eager to help, we formed a group called ECO — the Environmental Childrens' Organization. Our message is that children are the future, and the mess adults leave will be *our* home one day.

With help from the Environmental Youth Alliance (EYA), a network of high-school environmentalists, we got funding from our neighbourhood bank, VanCity, to produce three newspapers that were sent to Elementary schools. The EYA helped us a lot. We started our first project after Thom Henley gave a talk about the Penan people in Sarawak, Malaysia. He told us about these gentle forest people being pushed off their land by international companies that are destroying the forests and polluting the rivers the Penan drink and bathe in. We decided to raise money and purchase a water filter for them. From selling jewellery to baking cupcakes, we did raise the money, and finally presented the filter to a Penan man called Mutang Tuo when he came to Vancouver.

In the early spring of 1991 I heard about a huge environmental meeting which was to take place in Rio de Janeiro, Brazil. The United Nations Conference on Environment and Development — UNCED — or Earth Summit, was scheduled for twelve days in June 1992 and was to be a gathering of political leaders, business people and experts in the environmental movement. I decided that ECO had to go. The Earth Summit would be a perfect chance to get our message to people who have the power to make national differences — politicians.

There were three different parts to the 1992 Rio events: the Earth Summit, the meeting of official delegates and politicians from different countries; the Global Forum for non-governmental organizations; and finally, all the "parallel conferences," such as the Earth Parliament, which was held for those who had not been invited to the political conferences — those who have a hard time being heard but are nevertheless the most strongly linked to our Earth: aboriginal peoples, women, elders and children.

ECO registered as delegates to the Global Forum. Applying was complicated and my mom helped us out a lot. When I heard ECO's application was approved and that we had been assigned one of the six hundred booths, I could hardly believe it. We were going to do it!

We decided that four members of the group would go to Rio: Vanessa Suttie, Morgan Geisler, Michelle Quigg and I. My sister Sarika, Michelle's mom, Patricia Hernandez, and my

JOHN F. KIM, AGE 15

parents, David Suzuki and Tara Cullis would also go. But getting eight people to Brazil is very expensive. We had to organize major fundraising projects. My dad, realizing our determination, told me he would match whatever money ECO was able to raise. We also received donations from different foundations, like the Ira-Hiti Foundation in San Francisco.

Of course, we had bake sales and sold our jewellery that we made out of Fimo. The best sellers were our famous ECO-gecko brooches. We made hundreds! But still we needed a large donation to make the dream possible. So we held a fundraiser at the Vancouver Planetarium. We gave speeches and slides, explained our idea of going to Rio and finally made a pitch for money. Our first fundraiser worked! We raised $4,700 that night.

The enthusiasm continued, and we received several large donations in the following weeks. Finally, we raised $13,000 and with my parents' contribution we had enough to attend the Earth Summit.

Arriving in Rio was an amazing experience. It was the first time Vanessa and Morgan had travelled outside North America. It was shocking for all of us to see the choking pollution, the beautiful beaches that looked so inviting but with water too dirty to swim in and, most heart wrenching, the children living in cardboard boxes on the streets.

The Global Forum was like a huge fairground with tents for meetings and speeches and hundreds of small booths for exhibits. We worked hard setting up. We put up photos and posters, a beautiful banner and information about ECO. Soon the booth looked great. All day and into the night, people from different countries wandered around looking at the exhibits. There were at least two members of ECO working in the booth at all times. We gave out information in different languages; we all spoke English and French, Michelle spoke Spanish and I spoke a bit of Portuguese from my previous trip to Brazil. We met men and women from all over the world.

We especially tried to get our message out whenever a politician passed the booth. But they were rarely co-operative. Jean Charest, Canada's environment minister, came to our

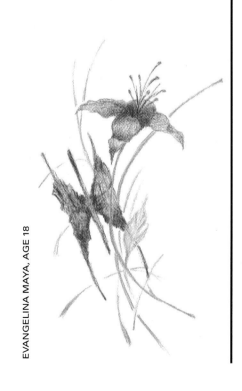

EVANGELINA MAYA, AGE 18

booth. It was our first encounter with a politician, and we waited for him to ask us about our organization and why we were here. Instead, he asked about school, homework and Brazilian prices. As he walked away, I realized we'd made the mistake of thinking a politician would take the initiative. Next time we saw Jean Charest, we pounced on him and told him our message straight. It's the only way.

My dad had been asked to speak at some of the programs at Rio. During each of his lectures, he gave ECO members the opportunity to speak for a few minutes each. We would squish all we wanted to say into the little time we were allowed. The first speech we made was at the Global Forum. The Canadian delegation from Ottawa happened to be there and we got a standing ovation!

Dad was also invited to participate in a press conference at the Earth Summit on a Panel on Education and Ethics. He had enough time to give Michelle and me time to talk. The response was so enthusiastic that some of the delegates even changed their speeches in response to our talk. Apparently, it was surprising to have children actually expressing their ideas at a panel on education! We got a lot of good speaking practice and each time we gave a presentation there was a great improvement in our public speaking.

We were interviewed by many different reporters. One of them, David Halton from the CBC, and his crew spent four days with us, putting together a news piece about ECO in Rio. We visited the *favellas*, or slums, of the city with David and met and talked with some of the street kids through a translator and social worker. For us, it was an entirely different world. There are children our age in Rio whose homes are no more than wood or paper boxes. These children have nowhere to go, nowhere they are wanted. They really made us think. The rich often take frivolities for granted and throw away things the poor desperately need. Poverty continues because people are greedy. We have to share, and question why some people starve while others waste so much.

The speech we gave at the Earth Parliament was a real turning point. The executive director of UNICEF, James Grant, was in the audience and he was so struck by our talk that he asked me for a copy, saying he was going to personally hand

We have to share, and question why some people starve while others waste so much.

it to Canadian Prime Minister Brian Mulroney when he arrived in Rio. Later, he told Maurice Strong, the executive director of UNCED, about us and our message.

Apparently, James Grant's support did the trick and ECO was slotted in for the Plenary Session of the official Earth Summit on the night of June 11. WOW!

Even on the bumpy, hectic taxi ride to Riocentro where the Earth Summit was, I went nervously over my speech again and again, making more and more changes to the already messy copy. My friends added ideas from their speeches to mine so that it would cover everything we wanted to say.

Three children spoke ahead of me — we were the only kids to address the official conference at Rio. The other children were girls from international groups. A fourteen-year-old Canadian spoke about the importance of education; a sixteen-year-old German spoke about the privileges of children from Western countries. And a fifteen-year-old from Chile spoke of the services that Third World countries badly need. Each speech was very good.

After the girl from Chile left the podium, the room quietened down again. I got up, took a deep breath, and looked out at all the politicians and important-looking people. I didn't know who everyone was, but I found out later that Senator Al Gore, who is now the vice-president of the United States, was in the audience. What I *did* know was that this was the important moment; all our fundraising and speeches and work had led to this. This was our big chance. What if I blew it? My heart was pounding so hard I thought everyone in the room could hear it. Taking a breath I plunged into my speech.

Hello, I'm Severn Suzuki speaking on behalf of
ECO, the Environmental Children's Organization.
We're a group of twelve- and thirteen-year-olds
from Canada trying to make a difference.
We raised all the money ourselves to come
six thousand miles to tell you adults you *must*
change your ways.

Coming up here today, I have no hidden
agenda. I am fighting for my future. Losing my
future is not like losing an election or a few points
on the stock market.

EVANGELINA MAYA, AGE 18

I am here to speak for all future generations. I am here to speak on behalf of the starving children around the world whose cries go unheard. I am here to speak for the countless animals dying across this planet because they have nowhere left to go.

JANE BRANDA, AGE 15

I am afraid to go out in the sun now because of the holes in the ozone. I am afraid to breathe the air because I don't know what chemicals are in it. I used to go fishing in Vancouver with my dad until just a few years ago we found the fish full of cancers. And now we hear about animals and plants becoming extinct every day — vanishing forever.

In my life, I have dreamt of seeing great herds of wild animals, jungles and rainforests full of birds and butterflies, but now I wonder if they will even exist for my children to see. Did you have to worry about these things when you were my age?

ESTHER CHOI, AGE 15

LIA BARSOTTI, AGE 17

All this is happening before our eyes and yet we act as if we have all the time we want and all the solutions. I'm only a child and I don't have all the solutions, but I want you to realize, neither do you!

    You don't know how to fix the holes in our
        ozone layer.

    You don't know how to bring salmon back to
        a dead stream.

    You don't know how to bring back an animal
        now extinct.

    And you can't bring back the forests that
        once grew where there is now a desert.

    If you don't know how to fix it, please stop breaking it!

JI EUN LEE, AGE 20

Here you may be delegates of your governments, businesspeople, organizers, reporters or politicians. But really you are mothers and fathers, sisters and brothers, aunts and uncles. And each of you is somebody's child.

MARK BRIDGER, AGE 18

I'm only a child yet I know we are all part of a family, five billion strong — in fact, thirty million species strong — and borders and governments will never change that. I'm only a child yet I know we are all in this together and should act as one single world towards one single goal. In my anger I am not blind, and in my fear I'm not afraid to tell the world how I feel.

SLAVICA CEPERKOVIC, AGE 15

In my country we make so much waste. We buy and throw away, buy and throw away. And yet northern countries will not share with the needy. Even when we have more than enough, we are afraid to lose some of our wealth, afraid to let go.

ROMUALD KUCIARA, AGE 14

In Canada, we live a privileged life with plenty of food, water and shelter. We have watches, bicycles, computers and television sets — the list could go on for days.

ESTER PUGLIESE, AGE 15

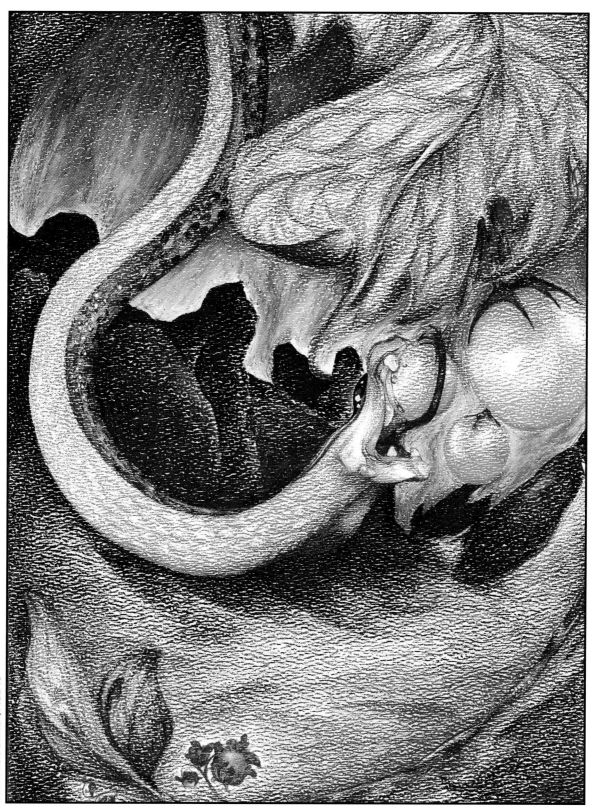

JULIA BOUGHNER, AGE 18

Two days ago here in Brazil, we were shocked when we spent time with some children living on the streets. And this is what one child told us: "I wish I was rich. And if I were, I would give all the street children food, clothes, medicine, shelter and love and affection." If a child on the street who has nothing is willing to share, why are we who have everything still so greedy?

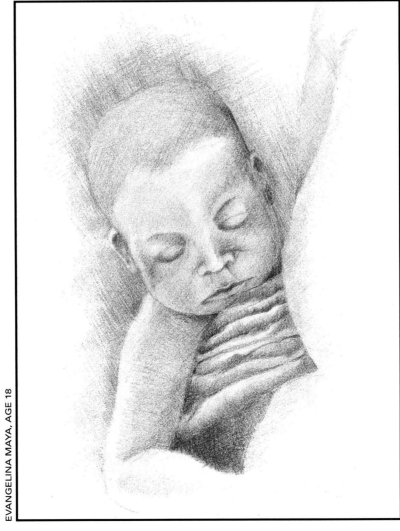

EVANGELINA MAYA, AGE 18

HEART LAVENDER, AGE 14

I can't stop thinking that these children are my own age, and that it makes a tremendous difference where you are born. I could be one of those children living in the *favellas* of Rio, I could be a child starving in Somalia, a victim of war in the Middle East or a beggar in India.

ERIC CHIU, AGE 18

I'm only a child yet I know if all the money spent on *war* was spent on ending poverty and finding environmental answers, what a wonderful place this Earth would be.

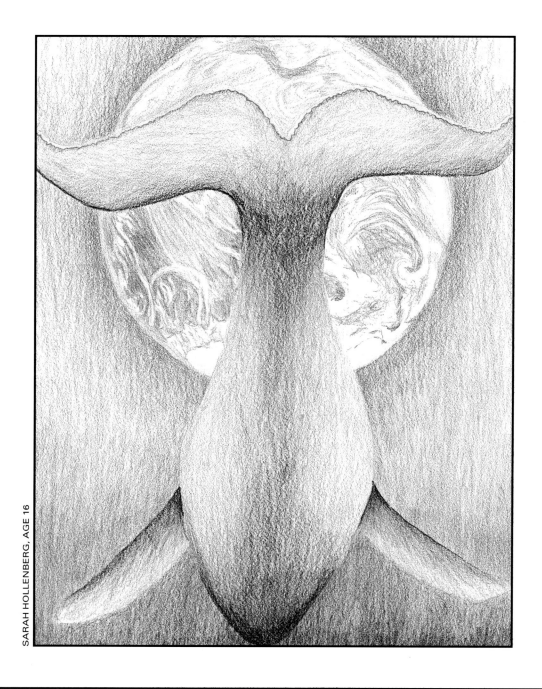

SARAH HOLLENBERG, AGE 16

At school, even in kindergarten, you teach us
how to behave in the world. You teach us:
    not to fight with others
    to work things out
    to respect others
    to clean up our mess
    not to hurt other creatures
    to share, not be greedy
    Then why do you go out and do the things
you tell us not to do?

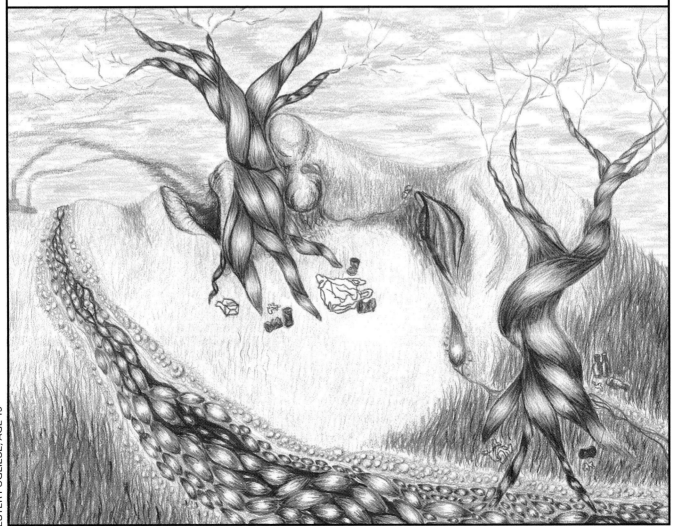

Do not forget why you are attending these conferences, who you are doing this for — we are your own children. You are deciding what kind of world we will grow up in.

Parents should be able to comfort their children by saying, "Everything's going to be all right"; "We're doing the best we can" and "It's not the end of the world." But I don't think you can say that to us anymore. Are we even on your list of priorities?

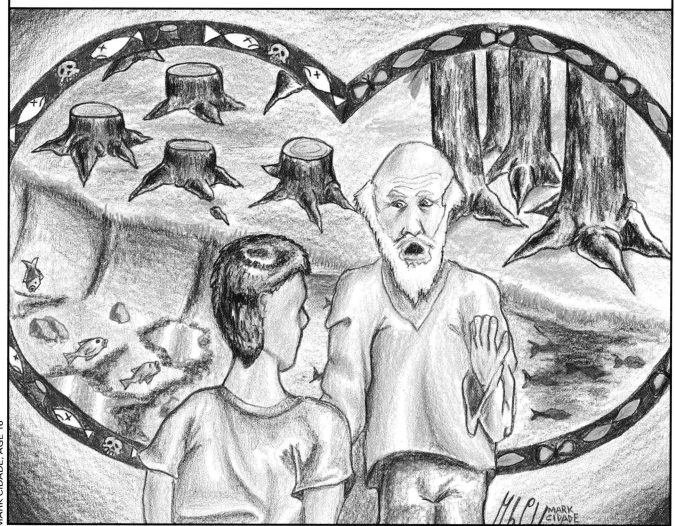

MARK CIDADE, AGE 16

My dad always says, "You are what you *do*, not what you *say*."

Well, what you do makes me cry at night.

You grown ups say you love us. I challenge you, *please*, make your actions reflect your words.

Thank you for listening.

JANE BRANDA, AGE 15

FABIOLA VALERO, AGE 17

As I left the stage with the other speakers, the audience rose in appreciation and tears shone in some peoples' eyes. I have never felt an adrenalin high like I did that night. When I sat down, Senator Gore came over, shook my hand and said, "That was the best speech given at Rio!" A feeling of mutual accomplishment gave all the ECO members new energy and I felt the tension of the last few days forgotten in the rush of realizing we had done it — together. We were congratulated by delegates from all over the world; the line of people shaking my hand seemed to go on forever. I felt as though I was in a dream.

Participating in the Earth Summit taught us that children can actually do something about the environment. I don't know if my speech made any impact on the decisions the leaders at UNCED made, but I know that it made people think. Maurice Strong quoted from the speech as he closed the Rio Conference, and the official UN film of UNCED ends with clips from my speech.

Working in a group is a good way to be effective because you can support each other and make more of an impact than you can on your own. My friends and I formed ECO because we knew we'd be stronger together. Together we learn more and generate better ideas for fundraising projects, for newspapers, and we establish contact with other environmental groups and try to raise awareness in other children.

I think one of the most valuable lessons I learned is how important parents are. Without their support, I couldn't have got as far as I did. Maybe the most important thing children can do is to influence their parents, because moms and dads love us! If your parents can help you, it will make your work more effective. And many of our parents have influence in the community and help make decisions that affect our future. When adults have homes, jobs and families, it's very hard to get them to change their habits — such as driving their cars everywhere, buying the latest fashions, wasting things and not recycling. People make all kinds of excuses. They say they're too busy or they can't afford it or they don't believe environmentalists. But when their own children tell them they're worried about what the world will be like when they grow up, parents can't dismiss them in the same way.

EVANGELINA MAYA, AGE 18

n fact, children can be influential on their own. Children *can* save forests that are being destroyed all over the world. One remarkable example I saw was in Costa Rica. I went to visit the Monteverde Cloud Forest. It's home to the almost extinct golden toad, and one of the most beautiful birds in the world, the long-tailed quetzal. I saw iridescent hummingbirds there five and six at a time. I heard howler monkeys and saw them scrambling above in the forest canopy, leaping from tree to tree. I saw moths with bright blue and orange spots beside beautiful little waterfalls.

The park exists because in 1983, a thirteen-year-old boy, Jerry James, showed a biologist a beautiful golden toad he had discovered that no one had ever seen before. People realized how little they know about the cloud forest and that there could be hundreds of undiscovered wonders hidden in Monteverde. To save it, in 1986 people began to buy land to make a park. In 1987, in a small rural school in Sweden, children were studying tropical forests and nine-year-old Roland Tiensuu asked what he could do to protect the animals and plants in them. This prompted his teacher to invite a rainforest expert to visit and they were so inspired the class decided to raise money to buy forest for a park. The small class raised enough to buy six hectares of cloud forest. This inspired children from countries all over the world to form groups and help save this special place by fundraising and sending money. Now, the Children's Eternal Forest is a large park. Children have helped to save animals and plants in a forest they've never even seen. By the time I visited the forest, children from around the world had sent in a million dollars!

In West Vancouver, a stand of old-growth trees below Cypress Bowl was slated to be clear-cut so that a golf course could be built in its place. Environmentalists were outraged and began to lobby the city council. Members of the Environmental Youth Alliance began to stand beside the highways with signs opposing the cutting of the forest. They stood each day at one end of the Lion's Gate Bridge during rush hour. Their actions were one of the reasons city council finally voted against the golf course. I have hiked through the forest and I enjoyed the spectacular trees even more for knowing how they had been saved.

A lot of

things you

can do seem

so insignificant

but when every-

one does them,

it really

adds up.

It's great to make a difference anywhere in the world. But you don't have to travel far to get involved. There's a lot you can do right in your own home. Get involved in the environmental problems that face your community. We've got to save our own countries before we can tell others to save theirs. Maybe there is a pond near your home that's being polluted or a park that's being changed into a parking lot. I think the biggest successes are often in the smaller issues where you really know what you're working for and can see the results.

You know the three Rs: Reduce, Re-use and of course, Recycle. An organization called WHEN (Worldwide Home-maker's Environmental Network), a local environmental group, taught my family how to cut our garbage down to less than one garbage bag a month. I think Reduce is the best rule. We shouldn't buy all the fancy wrappings. The most ridiculous example of waste is coconuts. To eat them you have to break them open with a hammer. Yet they are sold in a supermarket wrapped in plastic and styrofoam! Tell your local store manager that you don't like all the wasteful packaging.

Then there's air pollution. Take the bus whenever you can, and give up driving anywhere that's less than ten blocks away. It's a lot more fun to take a bike or rollerblade or jog or walk! A lot of things you can do seem so insignificant but when everyone does them, it really adds up. People throw away cups, milk containers, pens and so on as if it's OK to use something just once and then throw it away. My grandparents tell me they never threw things away just like that. My grandpa still saves string and rope and all kinds of stuff and they often come in handy. Why not think of "disposable" as unacceptable and try to avoid disposable things if possible? If you get involved, you'll find you can get your friends interested too and ideas will spread.

And of course there are a lot of things you can do in school. You can work to make the schoolyard a pesticide-free zone, and make it greener by planting gardens of wild plants, vegetables or flowers. You can plant fruit trees and berry bushes and then eat fruit you've grown yourself. You can raise bird-houses, build butterfly gardens and make planter boxes. It would be so great if going to school was like a visit to a forest or park. You can make a compost area for vegetable waste from the cafeteria. And ask the cafeteria staff if they'd be willing to consider getting rid of styrofoam containers.

Maybe you can start an environmental group with your friends. Together you can decide on projects in your school, your city, your country or in other countries. You can work on those projects and learn about other groups and projects and our global problems. You can raise money through different projects or lobby politicians. The most important thing for us to learn is that we are all a part of nature, and that we have to keep it healthy for ourselves and for our children. The world is an incredible, beautiful place — and will be as long as we don't take it for granted.

Fighting for the environment is very exciting. By working on various projects I've met wonderful people and from my experiences, I look at the world in a different way. I always have thought that when I grow up, I want to have an impact in the world. I want to make a difference. I want to do something. But I've already begun to make my difference — I think mostly because I *haven't* grown up!

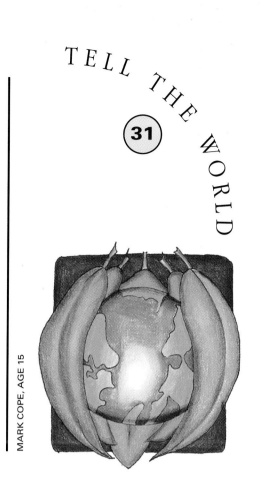

MARK COPE, AGE 15

DEDICATION

*To small people who get big ideas.
And to you who don't discourage them!
Thank you for supporting me.*

ACKNOWLEDGEMENTS

Getting to Rio was a joint child–labour effort. Thank you to the ECO (now ECHO) kids, especially the Rio gang — Morgan Geisler, Michelle Quigg, and Vanessa Suttie — who contributed to everything, including my speech. And to Tove Fenger and Sarika Cullis-Suzuki, who worked faithfully to support us.

These are the other wonderful people who made our dream come true: Tara Cullis, Harry and Freddy Cullis, Sharon Duguid, the EYA (Environmental Youth Alliance), Patricia Fraser, John Geisler, Jeff Gibbs, Herb Gilbert, James Grant, David Halton, Patricia Hernandez, the Ira-Hiti Foundation, Nancy Jackman, Thea Jensen, Ron Léger, Andrea Miller, Desirée McGraw, Ian MacKenzie, Raffi, Eve Savory, Maurice Strong, Carr Suzuki, David Suzuki, Bruce and Donna Suttie, Doug Tompkins, Susan Ward, and the Vancouver City Savings Credit Union!

Thanks also to Jill Lambert, my favourite (and first!) editor.

Thanks are due to the many artists who contributed illustrations for this book. We would also like to acknowledge the teachers from the Etobicoke School of the Arts, especially Rimas Paulionis, the head of the visual arts department, and Pat Cramb and Jeanne McRight. Thanks also to Marshal Bilous, James Sherman and Michael Amar from Central Technical School for their efforts.